S0-DYB-041

First published in Great Britain 1997
by Julia MacRae an imprint of Random House, London.

ISBN 1-58048-001-2
Printed in Singapore

THE ADVENTURES OF
THE LITTLE RED TRAIN

Benedict Blathwayt

Baby's First Book Club®

For Miles Butcher

THE RUNAWAY TRAIN

Benedict Blathwayt

Duffy Driver overslept.
Everyone was waiting at the
station for the little red train.

VISIT
PORLOCK

When Duffy was ready to start, he saw an old lady running down the platform. “I’ll help you,” he said. But he forgot to put the brake on and the little red train set off down the track . . .
Chuff-chuff, chuff-chuff, choo . . . choo . . .

Duffy saw a truck. “Stop!” Duffy shouted. “I must catch up with the runaway train!”
“Jump in,” cried the truck driver and off they went after the little red train . . . *Chuff-chuff, chuff-chuff, choo . . . choo . . . . .*

. . . until they came to a traffic jam.

Duffy saw a boat. "Ahoy there!" Duffy shouted. "I must catch up with the runaway train!"

"All aboard," cried the boatman and off they all went after the little red train . . . *Chuff-chuff, chuff-chuff, choo . . . choo . . .*

. . . until the river turned away from the railway.

Duffy saw some bicycles. “Help!” Duffy shouted. “I must catch up with the runaway train!”
“Jump on,” cried the cyclists and off they all went after the little red train . . . *Chuff-chuff, chuff-chuff, choo . . . choo . . .*

. . . until they ran into a flock of sheep.

Duffy saw some ponies. “Whoa!” Duffy shouted. “I must catch up with the runaway train!”
“Up you come,” cried the riders and off they all went after the little red train . . . *Chuff-chuff, chuff-chuff, choo . . . choo . . .*

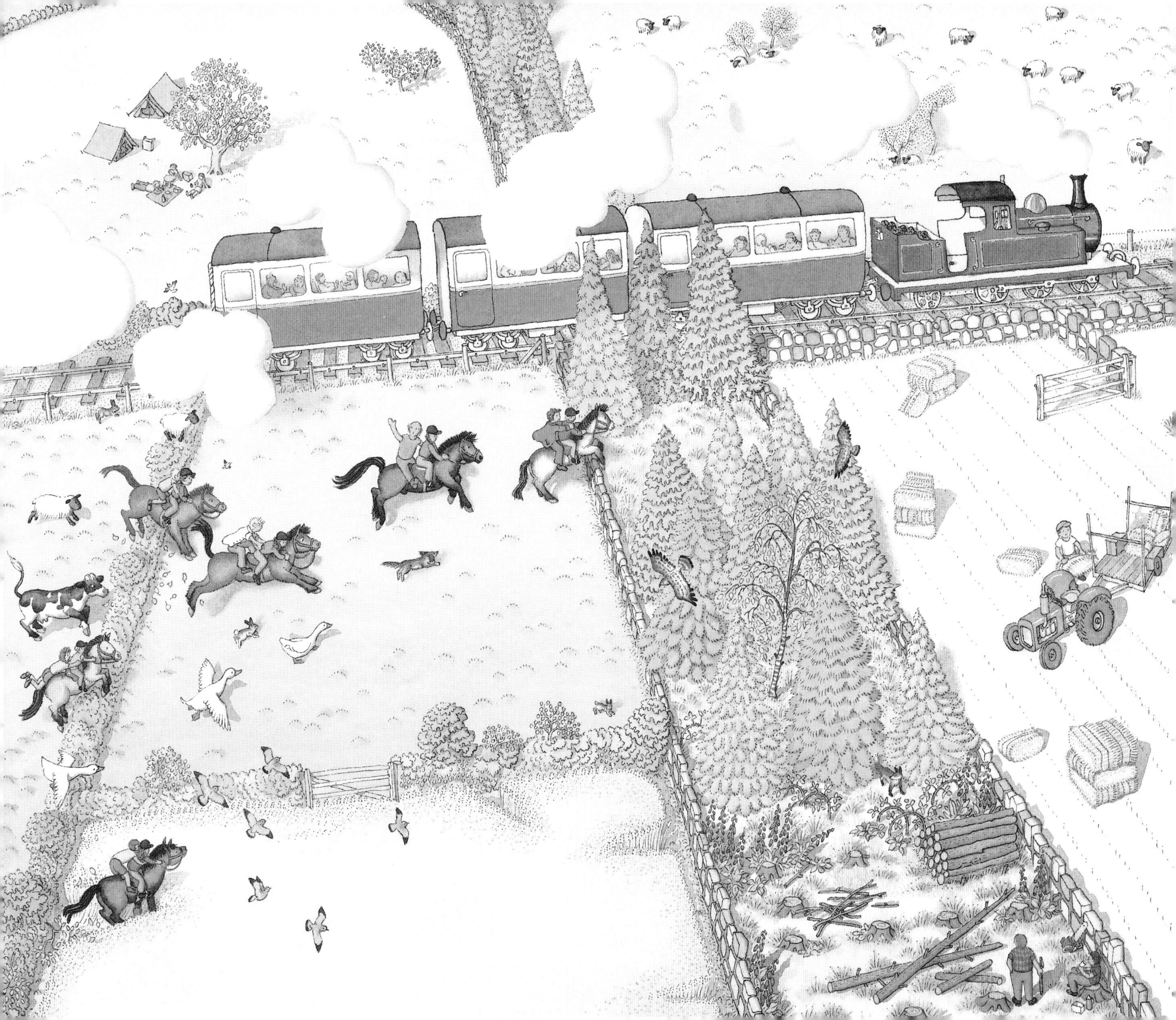

. . . until the ponies could go no further.

Duffy saw a tractor. "Hello!" Duffy shouted. "I must catch up with the runaway train!"
"Get on then," cried the farmer and off they went after the little red train . . . *Chuff-chuff, chuff-chuff, choo . . . choo . . .*

. . . until they were spotted by a helicopter pilot.

"My last chance!" gasped Duffy. "I must catch up with the runaway train!"

"Climb in quick," said the pilot and Duffy climbed in, while the truck driver, the boatman, the cyclists, the riders and the farmer all stood and watched . . .

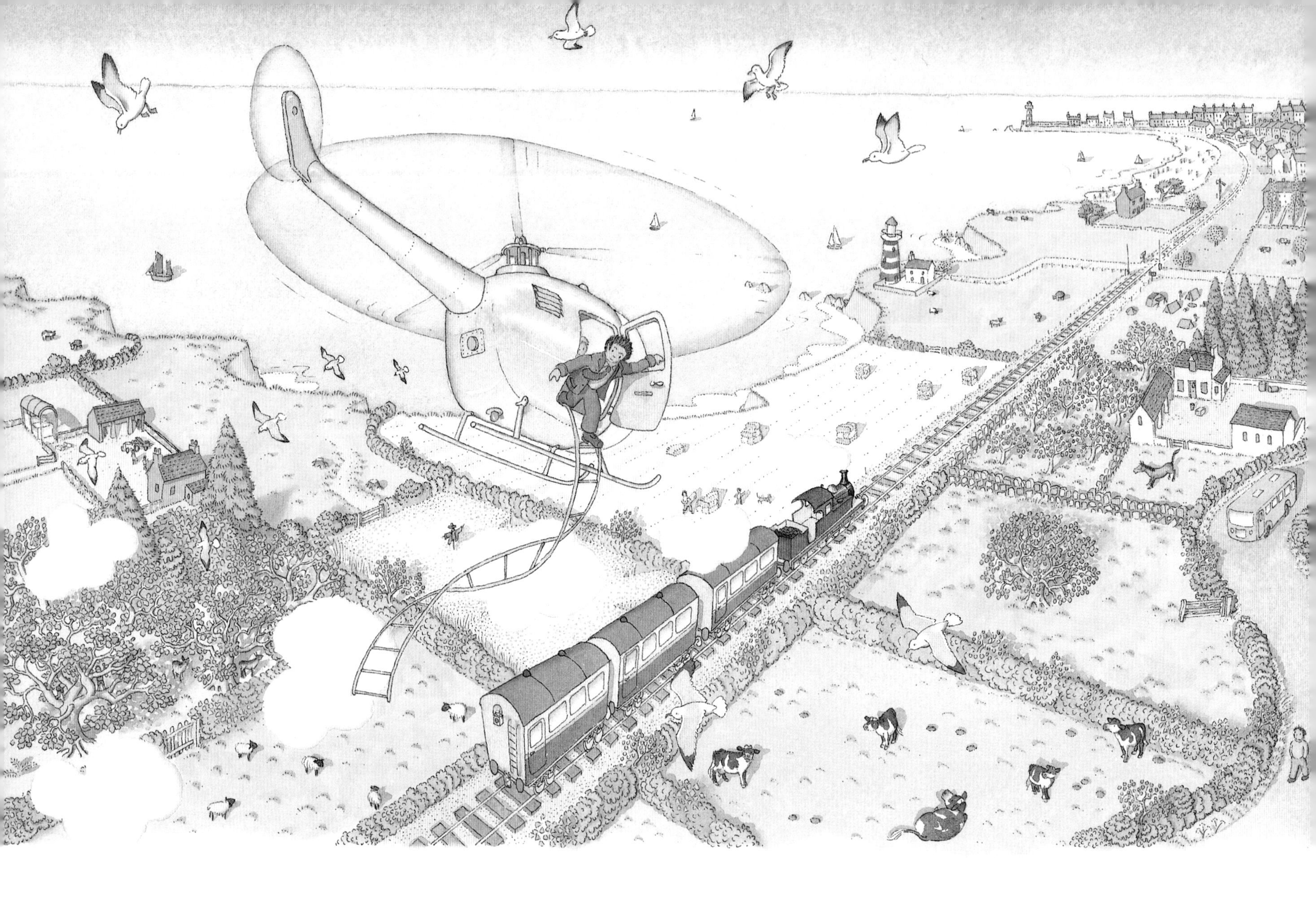

as Duffy caught up with the runaway train . . . *Chuff-chuff, chuff-chuff, choo . . . oo. . . oo*

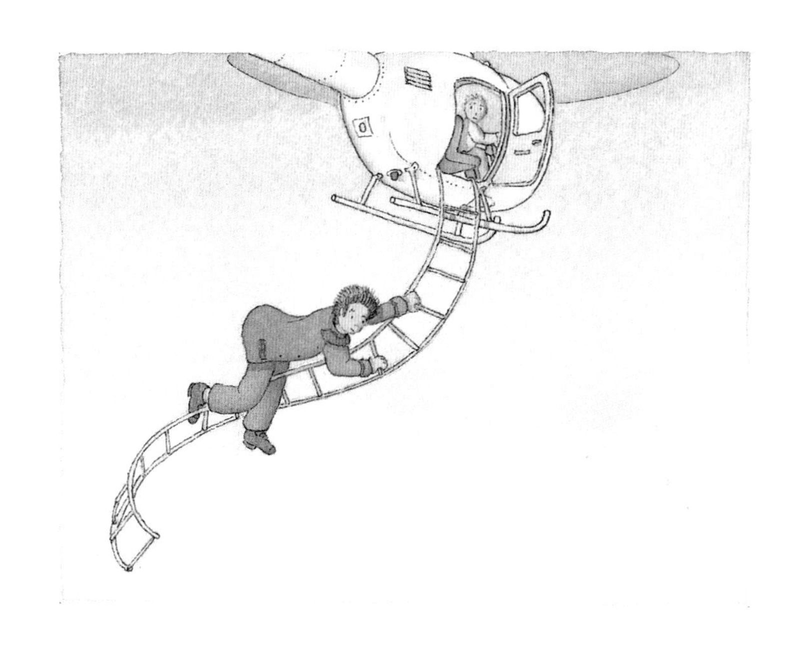

And Duffy Driver drove the little red train into the station at the shore and spent a lovely lazy afternoon on the beach before he had to drive back home again.

FOR LUCK

Chuff-chuff, chuff-chuff, choo . . . choo . . . choo . . .

For Matthew and Andrew

LITTLE RED TRAIN TO THE RESCUE

Benedict Blathwayt

One wet and windy day, Duffy Driver lit the fire in the little red train and collected three trucks from the goods yard.

The trucks were soon loaded and Duffy Driver and the little red train set off for Birchcombe village, high up in the hills. *Chuff-chuff, chuffitty-chuff . . .*

But as they came round a bend, what did they see . . .

Animals on the line!
Duffy put on the brakes with a *scree...eee...ch*
and the little red train stopped just in time.

When the animals were back in the farmyard, the little red train set off again. *Chuff-chuff, chuffitty-chuff . . .*

But as they came round a bend, what did they see . . .

The river had flooded the road!
Duffy put on the brakes with a *scree...eee...ch*
and the little red train stopped just in time.

They rescued the passengers from the bus on
the bridge and the little red train set off again.
Chuff-chuff, chuffitty-chuff . . .
But as they came round a bend, what did they see . . .

The wind had blown down a tree!
Duffy put on the brakes with a *scree...eee...ch*
and the little red train stopped just in time.

Everyone helped to move the tree
and the little red train set off again.
Chuff-chuff, chuffitty-chuff . . .

But the track got steeper and steeper and
the little red train hotter and hotter until . . .

POP! HISSSSS! The safety valve blew off the boiler!
Duffy put on the brakes with a *scree...eee...ch*
and stopped to let the little red train cool down.

Up in the hills there was snow,
so they set off again more slowly.
Chuff-chuff-chuff, chuu...ff, chuff...itty-chu...ff...
But as they came round a bend, what did they see . . .

A great pile of snow was blocking the line!
Duffy put on the brakes with a *scree...eee...ch*
and the little red train stopped just in time.

They all helped to clear the snow
and the little red train set off again.
Chuff-chuff, chuffitty-chuff . . .

But as they came to the last stretch
of line what did they find . . .

The track had frozen!
The little red train went off the wrong way.
Duffy put on the brakes with a *scree...eee...ch*
and the little red train stopped just in time.

The signalman poured hot water on the track and with a *chuff-chuff, chuffitty-chuff* the little red train ran on towards the station at Birchcombe.

POST OFFICE
BIRCHCOMBE
STORES

Everyone was there to greet them.
Duffy Driver blew the whistle, *whee…eee…eee*
and put on the brakes with a *scree…eee…ch* and the
little red train stopped at the platform just in time.

The passengers climbed down and helped to unload the supplies . . .

and Duffy Driver was given a nice, hot cup of tea.

Then Duffy got back into the driver's cab and after he had blown the whistle, *whee...eee...eee*, the little red train raced back home. It was downhill all the way.

OFFICE

Cuff-Chuff, chuffitty-Chuff . . .